First published in Great Britain by HarperCollins Publishers Ltd in 1999

1 3 5 7 9 10 8 6 4 2

ISBN: 0 00 198265-6

Printed and bound in Singapore.

WHERE'S TIM'S TED?

Ian Whybrow
illustrated by Russell Ayto

Collins
An Imprint of HarperCollinsPublishers

This is the farm where Tim's staying.

High in the sky is the moon.

Tim's got his jim-jams on.

It'll be bedtime soon.

Big kiss for Grandad.   One for Granny Red.

Tim says:

Excuse me,
where's my Ted?

Look behind the sofa.

Look behind the chairs.

"We'll find Ted in the morning. Time to go upstairs."

A funny thing happens in the middle of the night.

Tim says, "I think I'll see if Ted's all right."

This is the kitchen. No Ted in sight.

Pull

both

boots

on.

And into the moonlight.

Ben runs over.

Ben says, "Gruff!"

Tim says:

Down, boy. Ssshhh, that's enough.

Tim shines his flashlight into the shed.

He whispers, "Excuse me, where's my Ted?"

The hens start clucking, "Ted, Ted, Ted?"

Tim says, "Ssshhh-ssshhh. Come and look instead."

They tiptoe to the stable. They whisper to the horse:

Pacer says:

They creep to the cowshed. They whisper to the cows,

"Has anybody seen Ted?" But the cows only browse.

The ducks waddle down from the duck pond,

And the sheep flock along from the pen,

The goat butts in from the orchard,

All saying:

OY! WHAT'S GOING ON HERE THEN?

Then very, very quietly... they creep towards the sty.

They find the piglets fast asleep,

With mummy pig nearby.

But wait, who can that be in mummy pig's bed?

Is it a little piggy? No...

IT'S TIM'S TED!

Tim says, "Calm down, calm down!
Be quiet for goodness sake!
With all that noise you're going to have
Granny and Grandad wide awake!"

"Now excuse me, Mrs Piggy,

But that's my Ted, I think."

Mrs Piggy says, "Oh, snort,

I thought he was mine, being pink."

Tim takes back his Ted.

Says thank you and crosses the yard.

He wants to turn the doorknob.
He tries, but it's too hard.

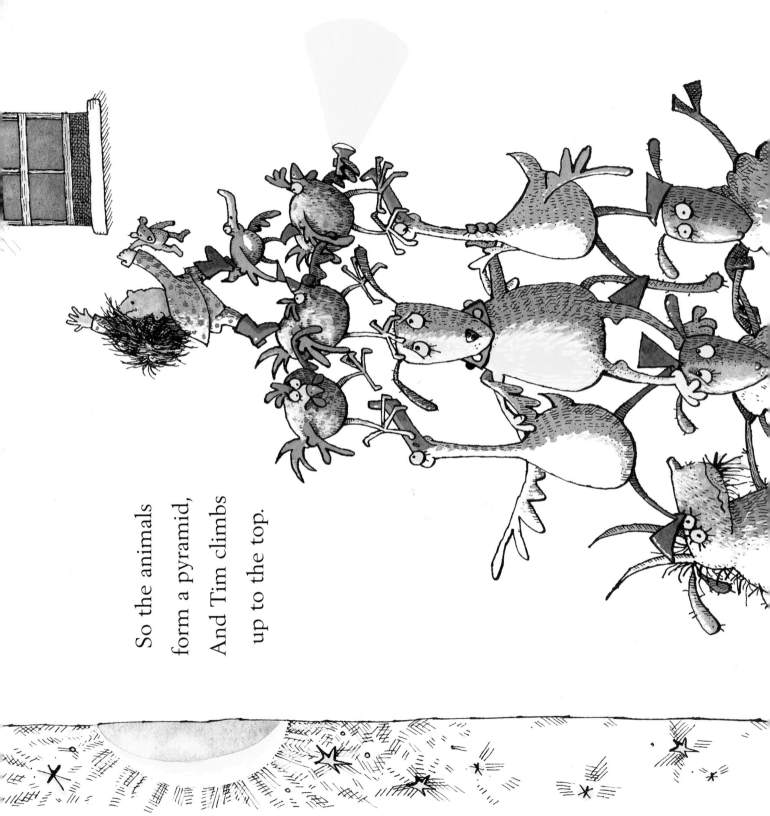

So the animals
form a pyramid,
And Tim climbs
up to the top.

Jumps through his bedroom window.

Back into bed, 2-3-Hop!

Granny says, "Are you all right, Tim?"

But from Tim there isn't a peep.

He's tucked up tight with his old pink Ted.

And – guess what – fast asleep.